THE
GODDAUGHTER
DOES *Vegas*

ALSO IN THE GODDAUGHTER SERIES:

THE
GODDAUGHTER
DOES *Vegas*

MELODIE CAMPBELL

ORCA BOOK PUBLISHERS

Library and Archives Canada Cataloguing in Publication

Campbell, Melodie, 1955–, author
The goddaughter does vegas / Melodie Campbell.
(Rapid Reads)

Issued in print and electronic formats.
ISBN 978-1-4598-2115-6 (softcover).–ISBN 978-1-4598-2116-3 (PDF).–
ISBN 978-1-4598-2117-0 (EPUB)

I. Title. II. Series: Rapid reads
PS8605.A54745G6323 2019   C813'.6   C2018-904884-0
2018-904885-9

First published in the United States, 2019
Library of Congress Control Number: 2018954144

Summary: In this work of crime fiction, mob goddaughter Gina Gallo
discovers while visiting Las Vegas that her identity has been stolen. (RL 3.2)

*Orca Book Publishers is dedicated to preserving the environment and has
printed this book on Forest Stewardship Council® certified paper.*

Orca Book Publishers gratefully acknowledges the support for its
publishing programs provided by the following agencies: the Government of
Canada, the Canada Council for the Arts and the Province of British Columbia
through the BC Arts Council and the Book Publishing Tax Credit.

Cover design by Jenn Playford
Cover photography by Shutterstock.com/Alhovik and
Shutterstock.com/trekandshoot

ORCA BOOK PUBLISHERS
orcabook.com

Printed and bound in Canada.

22 21 20 19 • 4 3 2 1

For Don and Ruth.

ONE

"I get it. You're sad about not getting married in your hometown." Pete gave me a little sideways squeeze. Awkward to do on an airplane when you're buckled in.

"It's not that." I tried to figure out how to explain it. "I like Hamilton," I said. "It's home. Sure, I'll miss the smog. How do people breathe in that clean Nevada desert air? It's not natural." I tried to make a joke of it. No point upsetting Pete with my sense of foreboding.

"You aren't worried about the family, are you? No one is going to object to us being married. They like me. Your uncle Vince gave me that Glock and all." There was pride in his voice. Probably I should be worried about that.

"You wouldn't understand," I said. Pete had no idea what would be waiting for us when we returned from Vegas.

I didn't know for sure, of course. But we're Italian. I am the goddaughter of the local crime boss. Reluctant goddaughter. I do my best to stay on the nice and friendly side of the law. You might even say it is an obsession for me. Certainly my wayward family thinks so.

The problem was, my Christmas wedding was being relocated to Vegas. Pete and I were eloping. We had good reason to do so. Our wedding hall had burned to the ground two days before the big day. This was not a particularly good sign. And it wasn't the first bad omen. Just before the fire, my great-aunt Zia Sophia had seen a crow.

That was never good. Sure, she was in Sicily, but omens were omens.

I might have been slightly superstitious. Not Pete. He just wanted to get married. So we'd escaped the next day and hitched a plane to Vegas. We'd kind of left everyone behind. This might be a mortal sin in an Italian family.

But there was no use ruining Pete's mood until we landed. Who knew? Maybe it would all work out.

I looked out the window. We were thirty thousand feet in the air. No crows around that I could see.

★ ★ ★

Two hours later we landed. So far, so good. The gods were on my side for once. We got off the plane with no incident and made our way to the baggage-claim area.

"You can sure tell we're in Vegas," said Pete.

I nodded in happy agreement. I'd never seen an airport like this before. There were slot machines everywhere. With all the blinking lights and dingle noises, you couldn't help but feel excited just walking through the terminal.

We followed the signs, and within minutes Pete was hauling the first of our bags off the baggage carousel.

It was just after lunch, local time. The flight from Toronto to Vegas had been four hours long. We had left Hamilton, also known as The Hammer, three hours before that. I was really looking forward to getting to the hotel. A shower was in order. And real food. Then we had some things to organize. Or, at least, I had some snooping to do. Pete claimed he had a place booked for the wedding. But he wouldn't tell me anything about it.

This was unacceptable. A girl needs to know. So I considered it a challenge to find out what Pete had planned.

I watched Pete lift the second bag off the carousel.

"Surprise!" a voice sang out behind me.

I whirled around. "Nico?"

There he was. All 145 pounds of lanky, grinning Nico. Complete with bleached blond hair and black eyeliner.

"WHAT ARE YOU DOING HERE?" I yelled in delight.

My favorite cousin raced up to give me a hug. I squeezed him back. Behind me I could hear Pete chuckling. There was a slightly unhinged quality to it.

"You didn't think I could let you get married without me." Nico pushed back from the hug and grinned.

"How did you get here?" I demanded.

"Oh, simple," he said. "I caught the earlier flight. Hi, Pete." He did a little floppy-hand wave.

Pete had both arms occupied with suitcases. He answered with a chuckle and shake of his head.

"I can't believe it! How did you even know we were coming to Vegas?" I asked. We headed toward the exit.

"That's easy," Nico said, loping along beside me. "I just had our mutual friend in the security business check flights for your name. You know how he is with computers."

I gulped. "Stoner hacked into—"

"Shhhh!" said Nico, putting a finger to his lips. "No names. The walls have ears."

"So you came by yourself?" I said.

"Caught the last seat on the flight right before yours. I was lucky. They only had a single seat." Nico sounded proud, even smug. "I've already been to the hotel. Just had time to check in."

"Which hotel?" asked Pete.

"The same hotel as yours, of course!"

Pete did that snort-chuckle again. I noticed he didn't ask how Nico had found out. Probably our mutual friend Stoner had helped. Heck, I didn't even know the name of the hotel. Pete had kept that a secret too.

"Well, really," said Nico. "Where else would you stay in Vegas but the newest and coolest place? Never mind that it's owned by the family."

"It's owned by the family?" Pete's voice had an unusually high pitch to it.

"Well, distant family. Somebody's great-grandfather married someone's great-aunt. That sort of thing. Doesn't matter. It's still the coolest thing on the planet. Wait until you see it!"

We made it through the sliding glass doors. It was cool, all right. I always think of Vegas as being hot because it's in the desert. But this was December. While the sun was bright, the air was brisk. I was glad I had brought my leather jacket.

Pete found the taxi stand and hailed a cab.

My cell phone made a *ping* sound. I took it out of my purse. "This is weird," I said.

"Pete, you get in the front," said Nico, reaching for the back-door handle. "Gina and I will sit in the back so we can talk."

"Nico, listen to this," I said. "I just got a message from Amazon on my phone, confirming my order from Linda's Luscious Lingerie."

"Oooh, Pete will like that." Nico waited for me to get in. I slid over so he could get in on the same side.

Pete was busy with the driver, loading luggage into the trunk of the cab. That was a good thing. He didn't need to hear this.

"No, listen, Nico. The thing is, I haven't ordered anything from Linda's Luscious Lingerie. I don't even know that store."

"What do you mean? Everyone knows it. It's like Frederick's of Hollywood."

Slam went the lid of the trunk.

"But I didn't place an order there, Nico. Why is Amazon saying I have?"

"Let me see that," said Nico.

I handed him the phone.

"You didn't place an order for the Naughty Nites peekaboo teddy and two pairs of crotchless undies?"

"Ick, Nico! Keep your voice down." The front passenger door opened, and Pete plunked himself onto the seat.

"Well, it should be easy enough to cancel. Obviously it's a mistake. Just go to Amazon and cancel the order when we get to the hotel."

Right. The hotel. I couldn't wait to see it.

TWO

About twenty minutes later I was standing inside the lobby, gawking in amazement.

"The NECROPOLIS?" My screech was drowned out by the cacophony of voices around us.

"Isn't it brilliant?" said Nico, flinging his arms wide. "Did you ever see such a great theme? And the execution is terrific!"

"Execution. Yup, that works, Nico. I could execute certain people right now." I wasn't such a fan of the theme.

Pete snorted beside me.

I continued to stare at the decor. Problem was, Christmas was only a week away. And a Vegas hotel, no matter what its theme, was not about to ignore Christmas.

So the lobby was a crazy combo of Christmas decorations and creepy hotel theme. I made myself look beyond the cheerful tree.

Blood-red velvet curtains trailed on the black-and-white marble floor. In the center of the lobby stood a statue of gargoyles with circular seating around it. Oh, wait—not a just a statue. A fountain! Fine streams of water spilled out of the creatures' wee-wees.

The rest of the seating in the room was fashioned out of overstuffed coffins. I squinted at the mural on the wall behind the coffins. Not one but—wait for it—a murder of crows. I was doomed.

Not only that. Those decorations on the Christmas tree? Candles. Mini plastic gravestones. And crows.

Nico could hardly contain his excitement. "Check out the name of the restaurant, Gina."

I followed his pointing arm. "The Crematorium Grill?" I groaned.

"Wonder if they only do well done," said Pete.

Nico pointed to a standing sign. "Look. A *zombie* convention! Just when we're here. Aren't we lucky?"

That was one way of putting it. The lobby was bustling with happy people who appeared to be extras from *The Walking Dead*. Some of them were wearing Santa hats. Which was seriously twisted.

"We seem to be the only ones alive here," said Pete.

Nico grinned. "And all the staff members are dressed as morticians! It's awesome."

"So that's why you're wearing black and white." I pointed to his white jeans and black shirt with the tails hanging out. "Usually you're more colorful. Like Pauly." Nico had a habit of dressing like a parrot. One parrot in particular.

"Speaking of parrots and their owners, Lainy is all excited to see you. She's doing a show tonight, but she'll call you tomorrow. Since she's your maid of honor, I'll be the best man. That is, if it's okay with Pete."

Pete's response was drowned out by the noise of the conventioneers. At least, I think the moan I heard came from a zombie.

Just to the right of reception was a shop named Dead Gorgeous. The window was a sea of blingy mermaid-style dresses.

I stopped. "Hold on." I pointed to a dress with blue sequins. "I am *so* going to try that on."

Pete laughed. "You can do that right after we check in." He took my hand and propelled me toward the reception desk.

"Better idea. Why don't *you* check in, and I'll check out that shop!" I was a girl on a mission.

Pete chuckled. "Okay. I'll drop the luggage off and meet you back there in time for the fashion show."

So now it was a "fashion show." Pete knew me well. "Nico, are you coming with me?" I asked.

He hesitated. "Actually, I'm supposed to check in with someone. I'll do that and then meet you at the shop." He gave a little wave and sauntered off.

I stared after him. "Well, that was weird. Usually Nico loves to shop with me. Wonder what's up?"

I found out soon enough.

★ ★ ★

Ten minutes later I was in the dressing room at Dead Gorgeous with a pile of shimmering dresses. Vegas was all about bling, right? Neon lights and blinking slot machines. Hey, I was only doing my part to keep the strip dazzling.

They had the blue gown in my size, so I started with it. I placed it over my head and tried to shimmy it down. It wasn't easy to get into. This worried me a bit. In my experience, gowns that are hard to get into are even harder to get out of. I hoped Pete would show up soon, in case I needed the cavalry.

I was just straightening up to admire the dress when a movement in the mirror caught my eye. I heard a *whoosh*, like the sound of a door being opened. The wall of satin drapery behind me billowed out.

"Hey," I said, turning. A large hand covered my mouth, and I was pulled back through the curtains.

THREE

I struggled and I kicked. Correction. I tried to kick, but the tight sequined dress didn't allow for much movement at the knees. *Note to self: Skip the mermaid style in case of future kidnappings.*

"Shit," said my abductor. "I'm not supposed to hurt you."

Well, that was reassuring. But it didn't mean I couldn't hurt him. So I chomped down on his hand.

"OW!" he yelled. "Son of a BITCH! Micky, grab her feet."

Micky whoever-he-was grabbed my feet, and the next thing I knew I was in the air. They carried me along a small deserted hallway behind the stores. I *hate* being carried. Almost as much as I was beginning to hate this dress. Sequins scratch, dammit. After all this struggling, my underarms were going to be a mess.

We passed another goon as we maneuvered through an open doorway.

"Aw, Ricky. You couldn't have done it any other way? Put her down," said a deep male voice.

Micky and Ricky? I suppressed a giggle. I mean, let's face it. You can't be scared of thugs who sound like a boy band from the eighties.

They plunked me down in front of a wooden desk. Micky left the room and closed the door behind him. Ricky stayed. His hand appeared to be permanently glued to my shoulder. The other parts of him were standard-issue Italian Stallion. Brown eyes, high cheekbones, black hair slicked back. He could have walked out of a high school production of *Grease*.

I turned toward the owner of the deep voice, who sat behind the desk. His face looked a little familiar, but I couldn't place it.

While he stared at me, I had time to look at him. He had a good-looking face, for an older guy. For some reason I thought of Dean Martin in his middle years. There was intelligence in the eyes, and a touch of humor too.

He sat tall behind the desk. I took in the upmarket gray suit jacket, the crisp white shirt with no tie, the solid set of his shoulders. His hands were busy, playing with a squeeze ball or something.

"Well, well. She's a looker, Ricky. Should have expected that."

"Take your hands off me," I growled at Ricky. He clutched my shoulder harder.

I made my decision. Showtime. To hell with the dress. I didn't care if it got ruined. No way was I going down without a fight. And these guys? They had no idea what I was capable of.

I swiveled my head back to the man who seemed to be in charge. "You want I should kill him or just hurt him a bit?" I said nonchalantly. "Of course, I can't be sure to get it right."

"Ha!" the older man barked.

I waited.

"Take your mitts off her, Ricky," he said. He looked at me. "You Canadians have a funny way of talking."

"It's our winters. The cold makes us friendly." I was doing my best to follow the family training we all got: Never show fear. *Never*.

"You sure got a smart mouth. Happens I don't mind that. Ricky, get her purse."

My jaw dropped. "You're going to rob me?

Poor schmucks. I didn't have more than thirty bucks on me.

"Of course not. Ricky, hurry up and get her passport."

I smiled and watched Ricky search through my purse. Pete had locked our passports in the hotel-room safe.

"Not here, boss," said the goon.

"Okay, driver's license."

This was weird. I decided it was time to bring out the big guns. "Probably at this point I should tell you about my uncle Vince."

"I know your uncle Vince," said the man behind the desk.

Crap.

I watched the goon flip through my wallet. He handed it over to the man behind the desk.

"The print is too small. Read that, Ricky."

"May fifth, 1988," said Ricky.

The big man looked up. "That your birthday, sweetheart?"

I was baffled. "Yup. You could have just asked me."

He stared at me now. I wasn't sure he liked what he saw. "Rita was right. So Marie is your mom. Sure looks like Marie did, I'll say that. Doesn't act like her though."

Marie? This guy knew my mom?

"Who *are* you?" I blurted out.

"Frank Portobello. Yeah, like the mushroom, but don't say it."

I got the impression it might be unhealthy to say it.

"I run this joint." He swept a big hand through the air.

By *joint* I assumed he meant the Necropolis, not the back end of the dress store.

There was a commotion out in the hall. A few shouts, and then something big hit the floor. For a few moments we all stood listening, transfixed. Ricky woke up first and rushed to the door. I was right behind him when he opened it.

Two guys lay on the floor. Micky was out cold. The other was holding his crotch and moaning.

"Your thugs need better manners," said Pete, shaking his right hand.

"And you decided to teach them some." I shook my head.

"You know this guy, Gina?" said Frank Mushroom.

"Kinda. We're getting married tomorrow." Wow, that felt good to say.

"Useless bunch of pansies," said Frank, shaking his head at his men on the floor. He turned to Pete. "Come in and join the party." He walked back to his desk and sat down.

"You okay, babe?" said Pete. His sandy hair was somewhat ruffled.

I nodded.

"Nice dress."

"Thought you'd like it," I said. "But it ain't gonna happen. These sequins are like knives under my arms."

I turned to Mr. Mushroom and made the introductions. "This is my fiancé, Pete Malone. Pete, this is Frank Portobello."

Pete raised an eyebrow. "Like the—"

"Don't say it," I interrupted. "He owns the Necropolis."

"Pete Malone," said Frank. He turned to Ricky. "That sounds familiar. Do we know a Pete Malone?"

Ricky thumbed his smartphone. We all waited. "Quarterback," he said finally. "Retired in 2011 due to he got clobbered."

Frank nodded. He seemed to approve of the football. Or maybe the clobbering.

"And you snatched Gina and brought her here because…?" Pete still cradled his right hand in his left. I hoped he hadn't broken anything.

"I wanted to meet her," said Frank.

It was my turn to raise an eyebrow. "Why?"

He gazed at me long and hard. The next thing he did was surprising. He gave me a wide smile.

"Because I'm your father."

FOUR

I was in too much shock to do anything but stumble and curse. So I did both.

Pete caught me before I fell. "Hold on there, babe," he said.

"I'm not fainting!" I said. Okay—I yelled. "I tried to move and my foot got caught in the hem of this dress from hell." The bottom of the dress trailed on the floor around me. This is what happens when some goon kidnaps you from a change room before you can put on your shoes.

"My fault," said Frank. "Probably I should have given you some warning."

I glared at him. "Sure. Like, maybe leave a phone message. Or send a scented note. How the hell do you *warn* someone that they may have a dad who never bothered to come forward before?"

Okay, so I was a bit pissed. The room went dead quiet. I felt Pete lower his hand to his pants pocket. What the hell—was he *carrying*?

Frank frowned. But he kept his voice level. "You don't know the whole story. Marie kept you a secret. I didn't even know you existed until recently, when Rita put two and two together."

"And when was that?" I had to know.

We were interrupted by more voices. One was familiar.

"Oh, dear. Obstacles," said the new voice. "Bruno and Micky. Just tiptoe around them."

"Does this happen often?" said the familiar voice.

"Nico?" I called out.

He appeared in the doorway. "Hi, Gina. This is so exciting. I've finally met my long-lost cousin in person."

A zombie clone of Nico followed him into the room. Same height. Similar lanky body. Same grin. Close-cropped hair. Eyes lined with black. Take away the zombie makeup and they could be brothers.

"Gina, this is my son Salvo," said Frank.

"OH. MY. GOD. You're my half sister!" said Salvo. He ran over and threw his arms around me.

Yup. Definitely related to Nico.

"Watch the sequins," I said to Salvo. "They'll cut you like lethal weapons."

He backed up. "You're right. They're fiendish."

"Are you the reason we're all here?" I asked him.

He put up a slim hand, like a stop sign. "Guilty as charged. When Nico emailed me that you both were coming, I told Rita. She told Dad. And then she told us who you really are."

The phone on Frank's desk rang. He picked it up and turned away from us.

"Really!" said Nico, clapping his hands together. "That is so Hollywood. We could be in a movie or something."

I glared at him. This was not the sort of movie I wanted to be in. Particularly as I had no script. How was I supposed to react to finding out I had a live father?

Mom never talked about my dad. Nobody did. They all clammed up when I asked. I'd been led to believe he disappeared from the scene when Mom found out she was pregnant. Nico and I had assumed he was scared of the family. Or that he'd had reason to be scared of the family. Meaning they had given him a one-way trip into the next world.

We'd been wrong on both counts. My father hadn't even known that I existed.

How weird was that?

I watched him gesture wildly as he talked on the phone. I tried to think about what this would mean for him. He must have been shocked too.

"Salvo designed this place, Gina. He's an architect," said Nico.

"You designed the Necropolis?" I was impressed. And glad to be distracted from my thoughts.

"The theme was Rita's idea," said Salvo modestly.

Fourth time I'd heard that name. "Who exactly is Rita?" I said.

"Dad's younger sister. She's our aunt," said Salvo. "She hung out with your mom when they both worked in Vegas that summer."

My mother worked in Vegas one summer? She had just turned eighteen when I was born. The jigsaw puzzle was starting to take shape.

"She looks a lot like you," said Salvo. "You'll love her."

"I'm sure I will," I said. One thing for sure, I was anxious to meet her. Rita could fill in the pieces that were missing.

It was bizarre. All of a sudden I had a new crop of relatives. Unfortunately, they were in the same business as the old crop was. I glanced over at Pete, wondering how this would go down. Like me, he wasn't a huge fan of the family business.

Pete looked at his watch. "Look, sorry to do this, but I have to dash. I have an appointment. Will you be okay with Nico for a while?"

"What appointment?" I said. Why would he have an appointment in Vegas?

He grinned. "To pick up our marriage license. No need for you to come. I preregistered online from home."

"Oh!" I brightened. "Okay."

"I also want to check on the chapel, so I may be a while."

Chapel! My heart took a little leap. "No problem," I said. "Nico and Salvo can keep me company."

"Before you go," said Salvo, "let's exchange emails and phone numbers so we can keep in touch. I'll give you Frank's and Rita's too."

"Good idea," said Pete. He took out his cell phone, and so did I.

After that Pete leaned down for a kiss. "I'll text you when I'm done." Then he left.

I turned to look at Frank. What was I supposed to call him? Now that was a good question.

He caught my eye and covered the phone with his free hand. "I have to take this. Tomorrow I'm in Chicago. Let's meet for lunch alone when I get back. I'll be in touch."

I nodded as he turned back to the call.

Frank was top dog here. I understood the demands of being at the top of the food chain. But this was kind of a letdown after all the drama.

"Well," I said to Nico and Salvo. "I need to return this torture device to the dress shop. Who wants to come?"

"I do!" said Nico. I wasn't surprised. Nico was always game for shopping.

"Me too!" said Salvo. He slapped a hand to his forehead. "Oh, wait! No, I can't. I have a meeting. Can I text you later? Or meet you somewhere?"

"Make it my room," I said. "I think it's registered in both our names. If not, it will be under Pete Malone."

Salvo clucked his tongue. "Silly. I already know that."

Of course he did.

FIVE

Nico and I returned the dress. No problem there. I assured Lara, the shop manager, that I would come back later to try on less lethal gowns.

Ten minutes later Nico and I were outside the door of my hotel room. It was a corner room at the end of the hall.

"I'm on the same floor," said Nico. "Just down the hall. Probably I should warn you. Em...don't expect the usual hotel room."

I shoved the door card into the slot. "I think the gargoyle door knocker gave that away, Nico."

The card reader flashed green. I pushed open the door.

"Oh, wow," I said.

"Is that a good wow or a what-the-hell-is-this wow?" Nico seemed anxious.

I grinned. "A bit of both." The walls of the room were painted gray. My eyes were immediately drawn to the side wall. I walked to the middle of the room and started to giggle. The bed was a king-size coffin, complete with brass handles. The mahogany wood shone, and the duvet cover was ivory satin. The headboard was a giant tombstone.

"Oh, my god, our names are on that tombstone!" I said. I dumped my purse on the duvet.

"Ah, the magic of modern technology," said Nico. "Truly amazing, isn't it? Did you see the bathroom?"

I followed his pointing finger. "It's that crypt over there?" I smothered another giggle.

"It's not as dark when you get inside." Nico peered in through the door and switched on the light. "Really, it's swanky and ultramodern, Gina. Just like the one in my room."

I was still processing the faux-stone mural on the wall. Morticia Addams would be at home here. I wondered what Pete had thought of it. I could tell he had already been here. Our luggage was placed neatly beside an overstuffed coffin divan.

I decided to try out the crypt. It was creepy in a fun way. The mirror had a dark gray, carved frame reminiscent of medieval castles. Skeletal hands held the toilet-paper roll. The toilet and shower were pretty much standard, but the faucet handles on the sink were cute little skulls.

When I returned to the bedroom, Nico was staring out the window. Happily it was a real window. It had a nice view of the strip, not a graveyard.

He said, "Well, that was an interesting meeting. Isn't every day you meet your own father."

"Yup. Usually only happens once. And most people aren't old enough to remember it," I said. No question, I would remember this day, all right.

Nico turned from the window. "Don't forget you have to cancel the Amazon purchase," he said.

"Right! I want to do that right away." I grabbed my purse and pulled out the cell phone.

The second I turned it on, it binged.

"Holy crap, Nico! There's another message from Amazon. This time about an order from Sparkle City Jewelers!" I stared at the screen. "A diamond tennis bracelet? Four thousand dollars?"

Nico grabbed the phone from me. He thumbed it a few times and then said, "Okay, this is getting serious. Someone has obviously gotten your password to Amazon. They're ordering things on your account. You've got to get in there and change your password immediately."

I sat down with a thump on the edge of the bed.

"Wait!" Nico's eyes were blazing. "First contact your credit-card company and cancel the card number you have attached to Amazon. If the card is canceled, the person can't complete any more purchases."

"That makes sense." I grabbed my purse and reached for the card in my wallet. "Nico, this is awful. I feel sick. My heart is racing like crazy."

"Don't worry," said Nico. He clucked in a reassuring way. "We'll sort it out. It's a good thing you caught it so soon."

I spent the next ten minutes on the phone. The friendly customer-service rep wasn't surprised by my call. Apparently credit-card fraud is as common as crows. Now why did I think of that comparison?

I clicked off finally and looked up at Nico. "That's done. They're sending me a new card."

"Good. Now go into Amazon and cancel those orders before they get shipped."

I nodded. My thumbs started the process to get into the website. "I'm really glad you're here, Nico. I'd be lost without you."

Nico sat down next to me on the bed. He reached over with one arm and gave me a shoulder hug that meant more than words.

A minute later I was still staring at the screen. "That's funny. It won't let me in."

"What do you mean?" said Nico. He peered over my shoulder.

"It says I put in the wrong password."

"Uh-oh," said Nico. "I should have thought of that."

"What?" I said. This was getting creepy again.

He frowned. "If they broke your password, they probably changed it. So now you can't access the account. Only they can."

"Cripes," I said. "What does that mean?"

He sprang up from the bed and started to pace. "It means you can't cancel the orders. At least, not by email. You'll have to phone them."

I flopped back on the bed, looked at the ceiling and groaned.

SIX

"Actually, before you do anything, let me phone Stoner. He may have some insight into this." Nico reached into his pocket for his own phone.

Stoner is a friend of ours back in Hamilton. Stoner is a nickname, of course. It sort of does double duty. His dad owns a company called Stonehouse Security, and Stoner is the computer whiz behind it. Which is all pretty amazing, considering his bad habit.

After a few moments I heard, "It's Nico. We need your help. Call me back when you get this."

"He wasn't answering?" I sat up.

"Nope. Probably still asleep. He keeps weird hours." Nico pocketed the phone. "Don't worry, Gina. We'll get this sorted out. In any case, they can't order anything more on your credit card. That's been canceled."

"I wouldn't mind a diamond tennis bracelet," I said. But I wasn't so keen about paying for one.

There was a knock on the door. Nico looked at me. "Expecting anyone?"

I shook my head. "Only Salvo, maybe."

There was a second knock.

"I'm coming!" I yelled. I propelled myself off the bed, walked over and opened the door.

A smiling bellhop faced me. He held a long box in both hands.

"Delivery for Miss Gina Gallo," he said brightly.

I looked down at the box, which was tied with a big pink-satin bow. "Oh, how nice!" I said. "Nico, have you got any money for a tip?"

Nico appeared at my side and handed the young fellow several bills.

"Thank you!" he said with a big grin. "Have a great day!"

"That was generous," I said to Nico.

Nico shrugged. "They don't make a lot."

I placed the box on the coffee table and ripped into it. "Roses!" I exclaimed. "Aren't they gorgeous?" I picked up one and breathed in deeply. Bliss.

Nico peered over my shoulder. "Red, long-stem. Perfect for a Christmas wedding. Are they from Pete?"

"They must be," I said. "Oh, here's the card." I pulled a small envelope out of the box and opened it.

"That's weird," I said. Nico waited. I passed him the card. "Read this."

Nico read the message out loud. "*Love, Ernie.*" Then he glanced up at me. "Who's Ernie?"

"No idea," I said, truly puzzled. "Do we have an Ernie in the family?"

Nico shook his head. "Not that I know of. Maybe he's from here?"

"The only people I've met so far are Frank and his sidekicks. Micky, Ricky and Bruno. No Ernies, as far as I know."

"Well, it's a mystery," said Nico. He clapped his hands together. "I love mysteries."

"I don't know that I do," I said. This was a bit much. Especially after the whole Amazon thing. I was starting not to like surprises.

"Maybe you have a secret admirer."

I moaned. "Great. Pete is going to love that." We just stood there, staring at the box. "More likely they just made a mistake. Delivered them to the wrong room."

"Except the delivery guy said they were for Miss Gina Gallo," Nico said. "He used your name."

"Crap." I put the rose back into the box.

"What should I do with them? I'd actually prefer Pete not to know about this."

There was another knock on the door. I made a mistake and went to open it.

A little old man stood there. He had gray hair and a great big grin.

"Hi, Gina! Oh, my. You look just like your photo," he said happily. He shoved a bouquet of flowers in my face.

I backed up and slammed the door.

"Gina! Peaches!" cried the voice from the other side. "It's me! Jerry!" The knocking continued. "Sweetie, open the door!"

"Peaches?" said Nico.

"This isn't happening," I muttered. I parked my butt back down on the bed.

"I really think we should find out what's going on," said Nico. He walked to the door.

"Don't open it," I ordered. Thank goodness I was here with Nico. He would never open the door if I asked him not to.

He opened the door.

47

SEVEN

Ten minutes later I wasn't the only one groaning. I was still sitting on the bed. Jerry sat in a chair across from me, looking crestfallen. Nico sat beside him in another chair.

Jerry was actually a really nice guy. He had a lot of money and appeared to be generous. He was about three decades too old for me, but that wouldn't stop a lot of women.

Too bad I wasn't the gal he thought he'd been corresponding with. Too bad for him, I mean.

"So let me get this straight," said Nico. "You met this impostor Gina Gallo on a website called Sugar Daddy dot com."

"That's right," said Jerry. "She was... well, she was wonderful. My ideal woman. It wasn't just the photo. I loved her online personality. She was very feminine and gentle. Kind and sweet."

"So definitely not our Gina," said Nico, snickering.

I gave him the finger.

"Definitely not like *that*." Jerry looked horrified. Well, at least he was beginning to believe I wasn't the same woman.

"Of course, I knew there was an age difference. But she didn't seem to care," said Jerry.

Of course she didn't. She was after money, not a relationship. I said it to myself, though, because the poor guy was suffering enough. Not only was he the victim of a scam, but he'd also just found out that the love of his life had never existed. How awful.

"So when she said she could meet me in Vegas, I was only too happy to send her a check for the airline ticket."

"First-class, of course," said Nico, leaning forward.

Jerry nodded. "What else, for my sweet Peaches? And the five-hundred-dollar fee for crossing the border."

"What fee?" asked Nico. "We don't have a border fee."

"Oh, I am such a schmuck," said Jerry. He lowered his head to his hands.

I was amazed at how small his hands were. No larger than mine. He seemed like a genuinely nice guy. I felt truly sorry for him.

But I was also worried for me. At least now we knew what was going on. Someone had stolen my Facebook photo and was impersonating me on a site called

Sugar Daddy dot com. This was identity theft on a grand scale. Thing was, how far did it extend?

"Jerry, I'm worried this might be part of a bigger scam. She may have conned other men." In fact, I knew she had. Ernie with the flowers, for one. "Is there anything you can tell us about her that could help us find out who she really is?"

"How do we know it's a she?" asked Nico. "The impostor could be a man."

Jerry almost collapsed at that point. His bones seemed to go limp. He flopped back in the chair, making snuffling sounds.

"Oh, that's just awful," he said after a few moments. "I've been corresponding with a *man*? Talking lovey-dovey with a *man*?"

"We don't know that," I said quickly. I tried to signal Nico with my eyes. "I expect it was a woman. Someone who knew just how to appeal to you."

"She sussed out my preferences pretty quickly," Jerry admitted. So he wasn't stupid. He was just smitten. Jerry sat up straighter but still looked shaken. "I think I'll go back to my room now, if you don't mind."

I exchanged glances with Nico. Would Jerry report this to the police?

He seemed to be reading our minds. "I'm not feeling very well at the moment. I just want to forget about all this, to be honest." He rose unsteadily from the chair. "I'm really sorry this happened, and for my part in it. I know it affects you too."

He kept his eyes off mine. I did the same. The click of the door told me he was gone.

"Poor guy. He forgot his flowers," said Nico.

EIGHT

After that depressing incident, I didn't feel much like going out. Vegas was party central. I wasn't in a party mood.

"What should we do with all these flowers?" asked Nico.

"Why don't you remove the tags and put them outside another door?" I suggested. "Someone will get a nice surprise."

"Good idea," he said. He got busy and left the room.

A few minutes later he was back.

"I'll let Stoner know about this impersonator on Sugar Daddy dot com. It may be related to the Amazon thing," said Nico. "So the big question is…do we tell Pete about this?"

"No!" I said. "Not a word." The last thing I wanted was to ruin his time in Vegas.

"He may find out anyway," said Nico cryptically.

"We'll cross that bridge when we come to it."

Nico yawned. "It's getting late," he said. His cell phone chirped.

I rose from the bed and glanced out the window. Twilight had morphed into full night. Not that it ever got dark on the strip. In the distance a zillion lights twinkled frantically, as if they were competing with one another.

"That was Salvo," said Nico. "I'm pretty beat. So I told him we'd meet him tomorrow."

"Do you want to order room service for dinner?" I said.

Nico stretched his arms and yawned a second time. "Good idea. I caught the earliest flight this morning. Had to get up way before dawn. Plus there's a three-hour time difference. So it's later than it seems."

Pete arrived when the food did. We munched away on the best steak dinners the Crematorium Grill had to offer. They weren't even burned.

Nico made his exit after that. "Catch you in the morning, cuz," he said. He blew me a kiss and then waved to Pete.

When he was gone, I turned to Pete. "Everything set for the wedding?"

Pete grinned. "All set. You won't get out of it this time."

I opened my arms to him.

★ ★ ★

My cell phone rang the next morning. It woke me from a deep sleep. I looked around to see why Pete wasn't answering it. He was in the bathroom. I groaned and reached for the phone on the bedside table.

"Hey, darlin', it's me!" said the cheery voice at the other end. "All ready for the big event?"

"Lainy!" I yelled into the phone. "It's so good to hear you!" Lainy is my best friend. We met at college. That's when she started her band, Lainy McSwain and the Lonesome Doves. Hard to believe that was ten years ago. She topped the country-music charts with her big hit "You're Roadkill on My Highway of Life." Now I only get to see her when she's between concert tours and gigs in Vegas.

"Yeah, texting and email just ain't the same. Say, I'm going to be tied up here most of today, but I've cleared everything for tomorrow. And hey! Have I got a bridesmaid dress that will knock your socks off."

We agreed to meet the next day at one. That would give us lots of time to blab our hearts out and get me dressed for the wedding. Of course, Nico would be along too. But that was just fine. Nico and Lainy are kindred spirits.

I clicked off with a big grin.

When Pete came out of the bathroom, I was already diving into breakfast. Actually, make that brunch. It was nearly eleven. Eggs, bacon, hash browns and coffee. All on a little tray with flowers in a vase.

"Isn't room service the best?" he said.

"I was born for this." I happily munched away.

"Say, would you mind if I went to the gym for a while? Checked it out on my way back to the room last night. It's pretty awesome. Punching bags and weights. I haven't worked out in a few days." He stretched his arms in the air as if to work out the kinks.

"No problem." I was busy smearing red jam on toast. "I'm meeting Nico this morning. And more relatives."

"More relatives," Pete muttered. Before he left for the gym, we made a date to meet in the lobby later, to see the sights.

I had a shower and blow-dried my hair. Today we would be sightseeing. This called for casual clothes and flat shoes. I pulled on black pants and a deep-blue sweater I knew Pete liked.

Nico bounced into the room while I was strapping on my watch. It startled the heck out of me to see the door swing open.

"Just me," he called out. Today he was wearing all black. Black jeans, black turtleneck and black leather jacket. The somber hotel theme was safe from Nico's parrot wardrobe.

"Wasn't that door locked?" I asked.

"Oh, that." Nico waved a hand in the air. "Salvo made me an extra entry card for your room."

"You're kidding." Honestly. This was a bit much. My new relatives were as bad as my old ones.

"Never mind about that," said Nico. His eyes were wide. "I just heard back from Stoner. And you're not going to like it."

"Okay." I sucked in air. "Give it to me straight."

Nico cleared his throat. "Remember when you had your credit-card number stolen last month?"

"I remember. How could I forget?" Mario, my doofus cousin, had sold my credit-card number in a scam the family had going. He was prone to making mistakes. Unfortunately, you don't get very far in the mob business if you steal credit-card numbers from your own family. Nico liked to say that Mario was out for a pee break when God handed out brains.

"Stoner says the person who bought the card number would have been able to find out your address and phone number.

As well as your name, birth date and other goodies. In fact, everything they would need to impersonate you on Amazon and Sugar Daddy dot com."

A feeling of cold crept up my back. "So all this goes back to Mario screwing up? Freakin' hell!"

Nico cluck-clucked. "That boy can't get anything right."

A worse thought came to me. "But Nico, is this it? What did Stoner say? Is this as far as it goes?"

"Don't know yet. We need to be alert."

I threw up my arms. "Oh, great. Now what's going to happen?"

Nico grinned. "I truly don't know. Isn't it exciting?"

I whacked him gently across the head.

"Hey!" he said. "Watch the hair!"

I scowled at him. "Serves you right for spending more time in the bathroom than I do."

Someone was knocking on the door. Nico and I looked at each other.

"What now?" I wailed. "Not another Ernie or Jerry!"

"I'll answer it," he said. I figured Nico thought he was protecting me in some way.

He threw open the door. A bell-boy-slash-mortician stood there. He had a large flat parcel in his hands. Actually, one end was resting on the floor, and he was merely holding the package upright.

"Delivery for Gina Gallo," said the bellboy. He hefted the parcel over to Nico.

I groaned. "Not more gifts from unknown admirers."

"Don't think so this time," said Nico. "There's a note taped on here. It appears to be from Frank Portabello. Here." He pulled it off and handed it to me.

"*Wanted to give you a wedding gift. Let's have lunch on Wednesday, just you and me.*

I'll mark it in my calendar. Frank." I read it out loud. Then I showed it to Nico.

"Interesting that he signed it Frank and not Dad," said Nico.

"*Dad* would be creepy," I said. I wasn't sure what kind of relationship we were going to end up with. But I wasn't ready to call him Dad.

"Help me rip the wrapping off," I said.

Nico and I worked together. There is something satisfying about ripping paper off a parcel. It's almost as much fun as popping Bubble Wrap. When we got done, Nico held the contents upright.

It was a painting. A black velvet painting of Elvis.

"That's weird," I said.

"Beyond weird," Nico agreed. We both gazed at the iconic painting of Elvis wearing a white jumpsuit. He was holding a microphone. It was the sort of painting that would have been really cool in the 1970s.

"Maybe there's some significance we don't know about?" Nico said.

"Beats me." As a wedding gift, this seemed bizarre. Sure, I didn't mind taking home a souvenir of Vegas. But...well, I didn't want to use the word *tacky* exactly. It's just that Frank didn't seem like a velvet Elvis sort of guy.

"We can ask Salvo in a few minutes. Rita is coming, and they want to meet us at...actually, right now," said Nico, looking down at his phone.

I grabbed my purse and jacket and followed him out the door.

NINE

"You haven't seen the casino yet, have you?" asked Nico. We were standing in one of the central elevators of the Necropolis, going down.

I thought for a moment. "No. Last night we came up through the service elevator."

"Usually they put casinos in the lobbies of these Vegas hotels," said Nico. "But Salvo thought the noise of all the slot machines would fight with the mortuary theme. So from the lobby, you have to go through a double set of soundproof doors to get to it."

I smiled. "But there's no way to avoid it, right? They make you go through the casino to get to your hotel room."

He grinned back. "Temptation. It's all savvy marketing. Now, be ready for a surprise."

After the dark and heavy theme of the Necropolis lobby, I didn't know what to expect. And then the elevator doors opened.

The racket of bells and whistles hit me like a physical thing.

"Welcome to Valhalla!" said Nico. We walked forward into a soaring four-story room.

"Holy cannoli!" I said, gazing up. "This is a tad unexpected."

I knew Valhalla was the name of Viking heaven. The Norse had a somewhat different interpretation of the afterlife than I was raised with. In fact, I was willing to admit that their version was a lot more fun, if these murals were anything to go by.

Lots of drinking, fighting and Viking versions of making little Vikings. Or it could have been more fighting. It was hard to tell. I tilted my head sideways to see better.

"There you are!" said Salvo, rushing forward. His arms scooped us into a group hug. "How do you like my little casino?"

"Love it!" I said. "Those costumes are to die for."

It was an odd mix. Staff members in this part of the Necropolis were dressed as Vikings. The customers appeared to be mainly drunken zombies. Did Viking legends include zombies?

Nico must have been thinking the same thing. "I think someone broke off an arm," he said.

"Don't be silly, Nico. Our slot machines don't have arms anymore," said Salvo. "They're all electronic."

"No, I mean someone left an arm behind." He picked up an abandoned zombie arm from the floor.

"Yikes!" I whacked his wrist to make him drop it.

"Time to meet Rita," Salvo said. "Tallyho!" He carved a way through the tipsy zombie gamblers. We marched through the double doors at the far end and into the lobby. It was refreshingly quiet, if a tad somber and morose in comparison.

"Probably I should tell you..." Salvo stopped walking. "Rita is sort of different."

Uh-oh. That was a warning expression in our family. Nico and I looked at each other.

"She's not dangerous or anything!" Salvo rushed to assure us. "She's just into some weird New Age stuff."

"You mean music?" asked Nico. His face was screwed up in puzzlement.

"Em...more than that."

Salvo led us into the Crematorium Grill, which was crazy busy. "We have a private dining room at the back," he said.

I had only seconds to take in the decor, which might best be described as Early Dracula-Movie Gothic. Then Salvo led us into a smaller room and said, "Look! There's Rita!"

TEN

My first impression of Rita made me smile. She appeared to be dressed entirely in veils. Lovely silk ones, in every color of the rainbow. Her flowing maxi dress looked like it could have come from Saks Fifth Avenue, if Saks had a hippie department.

My second impression? She was gorgeous. Her brown eyes were huge and needed no makeup. Dark brown hair curled down to the middle of her back. Her smiling mouth was wide with full lips.

"I'd know you anywhere," Rita said to me. "You look so like Marie." She reached forward to give me a big hug.

I hugged her back. It wasn't even awkward. For some reason, I got a good feeling all over.

Salvo frowned. "Actually, I think she looks a lot like you, Rita. Now that I see you together."

Rita's laugh was bright and bell-like. "Well, that wouldn't be unexpected. We share much of the same gene pool."

I guess we did. Rita was Frank's sister. That made me as related to her as I was to Pinky and Grizelda, my mother's sisters.

Rita pulled out a chair and gracefully sat down at the center table. We joined her. I gave her my most winning smile.

"Frank wanted to be here, but they needed him in Chicago for something," she said. "You know how they are. He told me to tell you he'd be back by tomorrow."

I nodded. I knew how they were, all right. You didn't say no to the *capo dei capo* if he wanted you in Chicago.

"Oh, dear," she said. Rita was looking at me strangely. "Gina, I don't mean to alarm you, but…" She paused.

"What?" I demanded. I had enough on my plate. What else could go wrong?

"There's something wrong with your aura," she said.

"My what?" I looked around me in a panic.

Salvo sat up smartly. "Probably I should explain. Rita owns a set of crystal stores here and in Arizona, in Sedona. She's very…" He hesitated, as if searching for the right words. "Attuned to the mystical world. Fault lines and all that. You know."

I didn't know. It sounded sort of loopy to me. But I wanted to make a good impression on my new aunt. So I focused on her comment.

"There's something wrong with me?" I said.

"With your aura," said Rita, nodding sympathetically. "I've never seen anything quite like it."

"Describe it," said Salvo.

Rita continued to stare at me. "It's muddy."

Nico snorted. It came out like a sneeze, but I knew him well enough to understand his reactions to things.

"Muddy," I parroted. Great. I had a muddy aura. What the heck did that mean?

"Sort of like there's a fog around you," said Rita. "I can't describe it well. But are you feeling okay?"

"I was feeling grand until one minute ago," I said. Did a crow fly in here or something?

"I wonder if it has anything to do with the identity theft," Nico said. He launched into an explanation of the nightmare I'd been through in the last while. First the Amazon theft. Then the immediate problem of the Sugar Daddy dot com impostor.

"Could that be it, Rita?" asked Salvo. "An impostor posing as Gina—could that interfere with Gina's aura?"

She nodded. "Definitely. It's really most interesting. I'd love to study this. But we need to help Gina get this sorted out, Salvo. This can't go on forever."

A cell phone nearby buzzed like a cricket. Salvo reached for his first.

"Nuts," he said, looking down at it. "I have to go. Apparently there's a problem at the zombie conference." He pocketed his phone.

"Anything I can do?" asked Nico. He moved to get up.

Salvo shook his head. "Not unless you want to clean up vomit and babysit drunken teens."

Nico sat back down. "Pass on that!"

Salvo sighed. "I knew this would happen. I warned Dad! With all that makeup our zombie guests wear, they don't look like their driver's-license photos."

"Ah!" said Nico. A smile split his face. "So you've got a lot of underage kids with borrowed driver's licenses getting plastered in the bars."

"Throwing up brains, no doubt," I added.

"You got it," said Salvo, rising from his chair. "I'll catch up with you later." He dashed out of the restaurant.

"Well, this is nice," said Rita.

I held back a chuckle. Nice wasn't exactly how I would have described the previous conversation. Nor the one before that. Nor the seriously twisted restaurant we were in.

"Say, Rita, you might know," said Nico. "Is there a family significance to black velvet Elvis paintings?"

Rita's eyebrows shot up. "Might be. Why do you ask?"

"Frank gave me one as a wedding gift," I said. "It was delivered to my room about an hour ago." I paused when I saw her face. It had softened into a look of pleasure. "I mean, it's a lovely painting and all," I added quickly.

"If you like that sort of thing." Nico sniffed.

I glared at him. Nico is a certified interior designer. Clearly, he did not like that sort of thing.

"*Well executed* is the phrase you are scrambling for, I expect," said Rita with a smile.

"That would work," I said, smiling back.

She leaned forward. "Well, yes, there is significance. Frank was a great fan of Elvis back in the day. And he likes his little joke. He obviously wanted to show that you are important to him, Gina."

"By giving her a velvet Elvis painting?" Nico squeaked.

"Well, yes. You see, she's family now. And Frank takes good care of his family. In all ways, including financially. Can you guess?"

We both stared at her.

She leaned forward. "Silly that he didn't give you a hint. I know he wants some time alone with you before you go. He'll tell you then, so I'm not really giving anything away..."

She gestured for us to lean in closer. "When you get home, take the backing off the painting. In the lower left corner you'll find some numbers."

"Numbers?" said Nico.

She nodded. "An account number and a password." She reached for her purse and took out a business card and a pen. She turned over the business card and wrote something on the blank side.

We both stared as she passed it to me.

"What is it?" said Nico.

I pointed. It was the name of a Swiss bank.

ELEVEN

Just about then Pete texted me. We arranged to meet in the lobby.

Rita had a meeting to go to, but she made us promise to save a day for her. "There's so much to show you," she said. "And tell you. About your mom and me, when we were together that summer."

"I'll look forward to it," I said, returning her hug.

The restaurant was still full when we left. I found Pete in the lobby, staring at murals.

I pointed to one. "There's a crow sitting on that tombstone."

"Why are you so superstitious about crows?" asked Pete, wrapping a big arm around my shoulders. "A bird can't predict when something bad is going to happen."

I looked at Nico and he looked at me.

"Let the poor Irish lad keep his innocence," said Nico.

We both nodded.

"Ready for a bit of sightseeing?" said Pete.

"You bet!" I said. "I haven't seen anything except the inside of this hotel yet."

"And there's so much!" Nico practically vibrated with excitement. "There's the Venetian, Caesars Palace—"

"New York-New York," said Pete. "Flamingo. The Eiffel Tower Restaurant—"

"Golden Nugget in the old town, and don't forget the Mob Museum," said Nico.

"They have a Mob Museum?" I shivered. "Not going there, Nico. No way, no how."

"Afraid of finding your photo on the

wall?" Pete laughed at his own joke.

That's exactly what I was afraid of. After the Lone Rearranger episode in October and my growing rep in The Hammer, it was a distinct possibility. And if not me, then several other people in my family whom Pete had met. But no way was I telling him.

"Let's get going then!" said Nico.

We linked arms like Dorothy, the Scarecrow and the Tin Man, and went out to follow the yellow brick road. The one lined with Christmas trees.

★ ★ ★

Three hours later we had seen a lot of the sights. We had wandered through the lobbies of most of the big hotels. I'd poked my head into several swish stores. Even I had to admit that the Christmas decorations added to the Vegas charm.

"You can never have too many lights," said Nico, wagging a finger. He was a noted expert in bling.

"Speaking of which, we have to come back when it's dark to see the light show at Bellagio," said Pete. "That reminds me! I have something for us to do tonight."

Nico grabbed my arm. "Velvet Elvis paintings," he whispered, pointing to a street vendor.

They looked pretty much like the one Frank had given me.

"Hey, I meant to ask you about that," said Pete. "There's an Elvis painting in our room. Where did it come from?"

Whoops! He didn't know about Frank and the painting. I wasn't exactly sure what he was supposed to know.

"Yeah, about that," I said, stalling. "Tell you when we're alone." I made it seem as if I didn't want Nico to know. Pete would back off then. And when he and I were alone, I knew ways to distract him.

"I think I've seen enough casinos," said Nico. "Time for coffee?"

I was famished. You can walk forever on the strip. Pete still had an athlete's constitution. Nico seemed to be mainly just nervous energy fueled by caffeine. But I was a typical Italian gal. Show me the buffet and stand back.

"Food!" I yelled out, like one would say *mercy!* "I need real food. Nothing stupid like a salad."

Pete chortled. He always gets a kick out of my appetite.

We were outside the Mirage. California Pizza Kitchen was beckoning, like the promise of water in the desert. I dragged the guys to a table for four and plunked my purse on the spare chair. A few minutes later, we had ordered.

"So," I said, looking across the table at Pete. "You have something for us to do tonight?"

Pete reached into his pocket. "Front-row seats to the Manipula the Magician show!"

Nico gasped. "Manipula? OH. MY. GOD. He's the best! Pete, you are awesome!"

Pete looked pretty pleased with himself. "I even got *three* tickets," he said.

"Well, it wouldn't be right to leave Gina behind," said Nico.

★ ★ ★

Pizza was yummy. We ate every bit of two pies and then headed out to the strip. Things were starting to liven up. Vegas by day was a happening place. At night and at Christmas, it was off the charts. Colored lights sparkled in all directions. It was like walking through a kaleidoscope.

The sidewalks were crammed. I kept a firm hold on Pete's arm with one hand. With the other I held my handbag close to my body.

Manipula the Magician was playing in a theater in one of the main hotels. It was about a ten-minute walk from the pizza place. Easy to find. Everything is well marked in Vegas.

Piles of people were pouring into the theater. Pete surrendered the lower half of the tickets to the usher. We made our way down an aisle to the front row. It was easy to find our seats. Yet another cool thing about being in the front row.

I sat down between Pete and Nico. This was great. Distraction was just what I needed. For the next two hours, I wasn't going to think about Amazon fraud, online impersonators, muddy auras or anything sketchy.

Tomorrow I was getting married! I smiled at Pete. He squeezed my hand.

The first hour went by in whirl of stunning acts. Nico had been right. Manipula was brilliant. No way could I figure out how he did those illusions. We clapped madly.

As the applause died down, the great magician said, "Thank you! Thank you. Now for the next part of the show, I need an assistant. Someone from the audience. Let's see…"

Manipula walked purposefully down the center steps of the stage. His gaze traveled along the front row and stopped. His eyes were huge as he lifted his arm.

"You." He pointed at me. "You're perfect."

Pete snorted. "Obviously, you don't know her well."

I whacked him with the back of my hand.

"He means you, Gina." Nico coaxed me with a hand on my shoulder. "Go, go, go!"

Manipula reached forward with his

palm open, like you do when meeting a new dog.

"Come," he said gently. "Don't be afraid."

Wouldn't you know he said the exact words that would bring me to my feet. Afraid? I was afraid of spiders and snakes. And maybe Aunt Miriam, who was scarier than any of the men in our family. But not Vegas entertainers dressed in funny gowns and capes. No sir. It took more than a Vegas stage to scare me.

I took Manipula's hand. Together we walked up the steps as the crowd cheered. I heard Nico's wolf whistle rise above the din.

The magician led me over to the standing mic. His face was rather ghastly with all that stage makeup. But his smile was warm and encouraging. When the applause had died down, Manipula let go of my hand. "Give them a big smile," he said to me.

I looked into the crowd and smiled. It was impossible to see anyone in the audience. The lights were too bright.

Manipula said, "What's your name, sweetheart?"

"Gina Gallo," I said clearly into the mic.

"GINA?" Three voices rang out from the crowd.

I stood paralyzed in front of the blinding lights.

"Gina? Pumpkin?" cried a shaky male voice.

"RUN!" yelled Nico.

I couldn't see him, but that didn't matter. When Nico tells me to run, I scram without thinking.

I was down the center-stage steps in seconds. Then I took off up the aisle. I could hear Nico behind me, saying encouraging things like, "Run, run, run, run!"

Unfortunately, Nico didn't give any instructions on where to run *to*. So I just kept going, into the lobby and out the door. At the sidewalk I bolted left.

"No, no, no!" yelled Nico. He slapped my shoulder, and we stopped momentarily. "Wrong way."

He grabbed my hand and pulled me along Las Vegas Boulevard. At the first intersection he steered me into the side street. A taxi stood waiting. Nico threw up an arm to flag it, and we tumbled in.

"The Necropolis," said Nico to the driver. "And can you let us off around the back, please."

I had to smile. Nico may have been Mob, but he was Canadian Mob. They know their manners. They always say sorry before they whack you.

Ten minutes later Nico opened the door of my hotel room.

"See? I knew this extra room card would come in handy," he said.

"Crap!" I slapped the palm of my hand

on the wall. "I left my purse behind."

"Pete will bring it." Nico pushed the door open.

"Crap!" I said. "I left Pete behind."

"Not for long," said Nico.

★ ★ ★

He was right. We didn't have to wait long.

I lay on the bed with my legs hanging over the side. Nico was draped dramatically across the only easy chair in the room.

The card reader clicked. Pete entered the room. When the door closed, he leaned back against it. He dropped my purse to the floor and crossed his arms against his chest.

"Will one of you kindly tell me what's going on?" he said quietly.

So we did. At least, most of it. I told him about the Amazon scam, and the Sugar Daddy-dot-com identity theft. Nico recounted the scene with Jerry. We both assured Pete that Stoner was working to get things resolved on the Internet front.

"So those guys at the show tonight were expecting to meet you here in Vegas," he said, shaking his head. "Poor schmucks. Wonder how many people this fake Gina Gallo scammed?"

"At least six that we know of," Nico said. "Probably more."

I just groaned.

"Anything else I should know?" asked Pete.

Nico looked at me. I shook my head. No sense alarming Pete any further.

"Can we call it a day?" I said. "I'm bushed."

Nico said goodnight and left. I got up to brush my teeth.

Pete followed me into the crypt. "I won't rest until you are legally Mrs. Malone. Far too many suitors waiting in the wings here."

I pointed my toothbrush at him. "It's my protection against showgirls."

He laughed and encircled me with his arms.

TWELVE

It was nearly noon when Nico phoned the next day.

"Here's the plan," he said. "The wedding service is at four. We're meeting Lainy at one, in the bar. Lainy will take you to the hair salon after we have a quick drink. Then she'll help you dress. I've arranged for a limo to drive us to the chapel. Pete will meet us there, of course."

I smiled. Pete and I had separated an hour earlier. I had no idea what he was doing at the moment, but he'd been given strict orders to vacate our room.

No way was he seeing this bride before the wedding.

Pete had yet to see my wedding dress. I'd hidden it well, in a special compartment of my luggage. It had packed down easily, like silky satin does. I'm not into Cinderella ball gowns. I don't like a lot of fluff. This was the sort of gown I knew Pete would appreciate. It had a low neckline, framed with rhinestones.

At five to one I met Nico at the entrance to Embalmed. Never had I been in a bar like this before. The whole thing looked like a morgue from one of those CSI shows on TV.

The bar was stainless steel, as were the tabletops. The surgical lights that hung from the ceiling were dimmed. White porcelain tiles covered the walls.

"Can you believe it? Look over there." Nico pointed.

I grinned. The bar itself didn't have bottles. Instead, there were jars with clear plastic hoses leading down to spigots. Most of the jars had poison labels on them.

It was pretty busy. All the tables were filled, so we sat at the bar. Nico dropped onto the stool beside me.

"I think that red stuff might be Campari," Nico said, pointing to one of the jars.

I was wondering what type of poison to order when Lainy rushed in. She spotted us and waved.

I had to smile. No one makes an entrance like my famous friend. With her big red hair and showgirl figure, she can rock a suede cowgirl skirt or designer duds. We got the cowgirl look today.

I expected a big hug and kiss. I got them, but her gorgeous face was a study in alarm. "Have you seen it?" she asked breathlessly.

"Seen what?" I asked. "The chapel?"

"The local news." She grabbed my upper arm. "Come on. It's playing on the screen in the lobby."

I sprang up. Lainy led us out of the bar. "Darn," she said when we got to the lobby. She pointed to the big screen on the wall next to reception. "They've moved on to something else. Wait a minute." She reached into her bag. "I'll get it on my tablet."

She pulled out a tablet and started poking it feverishly. I was completely baffled. What was so important that we had to leave the bar before I even ordered a drink? I needed that drink. It was my wedding day!

"Here it is," she said. She shoved the tablet into my hands.

I looked down at the screen. Nico crowded in behind us.

"*And in breaking news, have you seen this woman?*" said a deep male voice.

Now I really needed a drink. There it was. My Facebook photo! I gasped and listened.

"Police are asking for help in locating a woman going by the name of Gina Gallo, who is the suspect in a number of senior scams."

"Yes, Steven." The camera switched to a pretty young female reporter, standing in the lobby of another hotel. *"I'm on the scene in Vegas, where Gina Gallo has fleeced numerous elderly men out of their savings. One of her victims is with me today. Ernie, do you want to say a few words?"*

The microphone was thrust at his elderly face. But before he could say anything, a stout woman grabbed it out of his hands.

"I'll say something," said the not-so-pretty woman. *"It's despicable, that's what it is. Conning good men like my Ernie into thinking you love them. Pleading with them to send money so you can meet them in Vegas. You're a heartless cow, Gina Gallo! When I get my hands on you, I'll rip your face off—"*

The reporter wrenched the microphone from the woman's hands and turned back to the camera. *"All righty then. Gina Gallo has left a string of broken hearts in this town. Our sources say she selected her victims via an online dating site called Sugar Daddy dot com—"*

"Oh, no!" I cried. "My impersonator!"

"Stoner was right," said Nico. "It goes way beyond the Amazon scam."

"That's my Facebook photo! Just like that other fellow Jerry said, Nico."

"I figured it was something like that," said Lainy glumly. "This is just awful. How could anyone *do* something like that? Tricking poor saps into falling in love with you."

"There she is!" said a shaky voice behind me. "That bad woman on the news!"

"Looks just like her!" said another. Someone pointed to the lobby screen, which was replaying the clip without sound.

I turned to face a dozen angry zombie faces. "It's not me!" I pleaded. "It's someone pretending to be me!" My words were lost in the sea of yelling voices.

Nico clutched my elbow. "We have to get out of here," he said softly, close to my ear. "A crowd is forming."

"Hey, is that Lainy McSwain?" a voice rang out.

"Hi, y'all!" said Lainy. She stepped in front of me.

"Follow me," I said to Nico. Then I took off.

A roar from the crowd trailed me. This was unreal. I looked back once. The horde of angry zombies was growing bigger.

Dead Gorgeous was straight ahead. I raced into the shop, down to the back and to the middle dressing room. I whipped back the curtain.

"EEK!" shrieked a middle-aged woman in bra and Spanx.

"Sorry," I said. I leaped over her clothes on the floor and went through the curtain and the door at the back.

I dashed into the hallway behind the store. Then I stopped to see if Lainy and Nico were behind me.

"Hey!" yelled the middle-aged woman in the dressing room.

The curtain billowed out. Nico spilled into the hallway.

"Keep going," he said, getting his balance back. "Lainy is trying to hold the crowd by giving autographs."

It helps to have a best friend who's a country-music star. God bless her, this wasn't the first time she had distracted a crowd for me.

We raced down the hall. At Frank Portobello's back office I peered inside, but it was empty. No help there. I continued on to the service elevator. We dashed in. Nico pushed the button for our floor. I tried to catch my breath.

When the elevator door opened, Nico poked out his head and looked this way and that. Then he gestured with his hand. "Come on. The coast is clear."

We speed-shuffled down the hall to the room at the end. I swiped my card in the reader, and we stumbled into the room.

I threw my purse on the bed and flopped down. "Nico, what am I going to *do*? How am I going to get to the chapel without being seen?" I needed a huge scarf to wrap around my head. And big sunglasses. I had neither.

Nico slammed the door shut. He leaned back against it and ran his hand through his hair. That seemed to give him an idea, because he kept staring at his hand after.

"Here's another thing I've just thought of," said Nico. "Oh, dear. This makes it worse."

"What? What could possibly be worse?"

Nico looked glum. "What if they've alerted airport security to keep a watch out for Gina Gallo?"

And just like that, it got worse.

"Oh, no! They'll catch me when I use my passport. We were planning to fly back home on Friday!" I waved my arms in the air. "What am I going to do?"

Stuck in Vegas forever? What would Pete say?

"We have to find a way to kill off your impostor," said Nico, pacing now.

I sat up smartly. "Going down for murder one makes it better?"

"Not *really* kill her," said Nico. "Just make it seem like she doesn't exist anymore."

"You're going to kill her. At a zombie convention," I said. "How original is that?"

Nico sat down beside me on the bed. He leaned his elbows on his knees and put his head in his hands.

"How soon can I get my name changed to Gina Malone?" I said.

"Not soon enough. You have to do that from Canada."

"*Why* did I have to go and use my real passport this time?" I don't often admit to it, but here's the thing. I have more than one passport. We all do, in the family. It's a precaution. Let me leave it at that.

"You had to, Gina. Don't beat yourself up about that. You had to provide proof of identity in order to get married in your real name." Nico patted my hand. "It's just bad luck that Mario screwed up on the credit-card scam. I mean, it's kind of ironic. Your impostor used our scam to implicate you in their scam."

I groaned out loud.

"I mean, you're awfully pretty," Nico said quickly. "I can see why they thought your photo would be a honey trap."

A few minutes passed. My brain was

like a whirligig. How was I going to get out of the country? How was I going to escape the zombie hordes? Even worse, what was I going to tell Pete?

Pete! Who would be waiting at the chapel, all alone, if I couldn't get out of here.

Now I was mad. The dirty rat! *Two* dirty rats! First Mario, and then the fink who stole my identity.

"I'm going to kill Mario when I get back," I said. My hands were balled into fists. "I'm going to take a gun and shoot him through his mangy heart. Then I'm going to run him over with a steamroller to make sure."

"That can wait," said Nico reasonably. "First, let's concentrate on getting you married and back home."

Nico paced while I planned more revenge scenarios. Boiling oil? Too old school. Poison? Not dramatic enough.

Nico stopped pacing. His face brightened. "Wait a minute. I may be able to take care of it."

"How?"

He smiled now. "I have to make a phone call. Leave it to me."

I was happy to do that. I had enough to worry about right here, right now. My wedding was at four o'clock!

But an idea was brewing in my head. This impostor was not going to get away with it. No way. I wasn't the sort of girl who just let people stomp all over her. I would fight back.

This idea was clever. It would tie things up full circle. And it occurred to me that I had the sort of connections who could help. First, I'd need our friendly computer hacker/ whiz. Next, I might just call on my somewhat sketchy relatives. Just this one time.

"Nico, I may have a plan. A cunning plan," I said. "Can you get Stoner back on the phone? Or at least connect me to his voice mail?"

"Sure," said Nico, arching an eyebrow. "Are you going to tell me why?"

I told him. And then I told Stoner, when Nico got us connected on the phone. Stoner assured me it could be done. He'd get on it right away and report back.

I breathed a sigh of relief.

"Back to square one," I said. "How am I going to get from here to the chapel? I need a disguise."

"How do you feel about becoming a redhead?" said Nico.

"Dye my hair?" I squeaked. "On my wedding day?"

"POLICE!" yelled a voice in the hall.

And that's when the door exploded.

THIRTEEN

It didn't explode, exactly. More like it was murdered. WHAM! It pounded against the wall. Then it hung from one hinge, teetered for a few seconds and finally keeled over, dead on the floor.

"You know that wasn't locked," said Nico.

Two cops stepped over it. One was big all over, with short gray hair. The other was tall, thin and younger. The thin one was holding his arm and wincing.

"You could have just knocked." Nico tsk-tsked.

They ignored him. Instead, they both glared at me. "Are you Gina Gallo?" demanded the big one.

I gulped. "I'm the *real* Gina Gallo," I said. "Not the fake one that's been on the news."

"Sure, sister," said the skinny cop. "You can tell us all about it at the station."

Crap. The thin dude looked a lot like my cop nemesis at home. "Your last name wouldn't happen to be Spenser, would it?" I asked him.

His face went snarly. "That one of your victims?"

I moaned and looked over at Nico. "Go with them," he said. "Tell them everything, including the credit-card and Amazon fraud."

"Find Pete!" I said as I walked out the door. "Don't let him think I'm running out on him!"

"I'll tell Salvo and Frank. They'll know what to do," Nico yelled after us.

★ ★ ★

We were in the police car, driving down the strip, when the thin cop pointed out the window. "Why are there so many crows hanging around? We don't usually get crows right in town."

I banged my head on the back of the seat in front of me.

★ ★ ★

I hate cop shops. Which is really unfortunate, since I tend to visit them a lot.

This one was standard issue, gray and dismal. I find they all use the same interior decorator. Not only that, but all stations smell the same. Old pizza and stale coffee. Another thing I hate? They're noisy. Phones are constantly ringing. This station was especially noisy, as it was filled with customers.

Someone had taken the time to put up a spindly fake Christmas tree in the corner. It had some dollar-store decorations on it. Mainly plastic toy pistols in bright fluorescent colors. Orange, green, yellow and pink. Cop humor.

The big cop told me to sit on a steel bench and wait. I plunked my butt down. An older woman immediately to my right looked over.

"You new here, honey? Never seen you before."

I smiled sadly and said, "Hi. I'm from Canada."

My benchmate nodded. She appeared to be about fifty years old. She wore a pink leather miniskirt and a skimpy pink T-shirt. Her bra size seemed too big for her dress size, if you get my drift. She had bleached blond hair, and her colorful face owed a lot to Revlon. It was pretty clear she had spent a long time in a certain career. It was also obvious that she thought I shared her line of work.

"Goin' for the 'girlfriend experience' look, are you? Nice and classy. Good for you. I couldn't pull it off anymore." She patted my arm.

I almost groaned out loud. As if things weren't bad enough. Now I was being taken for a hooker on the strip. On my wedding day! I wanted to cry. Where was Aunt Miriam when I needed her?

The big cop came over and gestured with his arm. "Come on, Ms. Gallo. Interview time."

"Be nice to her, Bill. It's Christmas! And she's new in town," said my new friend.

"Shirley, you're just too naïve for your own good, you know that?" said Bill, shaking his head. "You always pick the winners. This one is bad, through and through."

"Hey!" I said. "No, I'm not. I'm…" What was I? Not good, exactly. I was stumped.

Bill reached for my arm. "Come on. We have a nice little interview room with your name on it."

"Um, Bill?" said a female officer behind the counter. "You need to come here for a minute first."

While Bill went to the counter, I gazed glumly at the corkboard behind it. Wanted posters. I shivered and looked for my own face. Phew. At least my Facebook photo wasn't on there yet.

Bill and the officer behind the counter were having a heated discussion. Why were they taking so long? Every now and then Bill glanced over at me. His face was in permanent-frown mode. My cell phone binged. I looked down at the email. It was from Stoner. The corners of my mouth turned up in a smile. My weird, nerdy friend had come through. Not only that, but the result of Stoner's...um...*research* proved that the gods were smiling on me for once.

I thanked my friend profusely by email. A steak dinner out would be coming to Stoner. I'd also provide special treats for his faithful companion, Toke, the giant black poodle with a Mohawk hairdo.

Funny how things work out. I guess I might have predicted it. Anyhow, no need to involve the family back home. I forwarded the message to my new relatives, Salvo and Frank, with an explanation.

I looked up from my phone to find the place still packed. Someone else's name was called. I watched as another officer escorted the unlucky customer into the back.

Then I started to fret. I had already missed my hair appointment. I should be getting dressed for the big event. Meanwhile, the big clock on the wall continued to mark off time.

"Oh, no!" I cried. "It's after three!" I had to get out of there!

"What's wrong, sugar?" said my bench-mate.

"I have to be at the chapel in less than an hour!" I said. "I'm getting married!" And then I burst into tears.

"Oh, poo, sweetie. Here, let me think of something." Shirley put her arm around me. "There must be something we can do."

We spent another few minutes like that, me quietly sniffling into her shoulder.

Finally Shirley raised her head. "How about I create a distraction? And you make a run for it."

I looked up. "But how?"

The corners of her mouth turned up in a grin. "The way that always works."

Her arms released me. Before I could say anything, Shirley stood up. She walked over to the counter and turned around. She reached down with both hands and pulled her T-shirt over her head. Then she threw it at a handsome young cop who had just come in the front door. It hit him square in the face. The other cops looked gobsmacked.

"Yee-haw!" she whooped. All eyes were turned on her now. As if on cue, Shirley reached behind her and undid the hooks of her Wonderbra.

"Hey, boys, it's hot in here. Ain't it hot?" She twirled the bra around her head like a lasso.

My new friend was a pro, all right. The room erupted in yells and cusswords.

"Shirley, what the hell kind of..." Bill charged out from behind the counter. "Jesus Christ!" He tried to reach for the flying bra without actually touching Shirley. That was tricky. A lot of Shirley was bobbling around uncontrollably. It was mesmerizing. I could hardly move my eyes away. Thankfully, I wasn't the only one.

Bill was on a mission though. He caught one strap of the bra as it passed through the air, and that started a tug-of-war.

It was the perfect distraction. Cops and suspects started calling odds. This was Vegas, after all.

God bless Shirley and Wonderbra. I silently made my way to the front and started sneaking toward the door.

I never made it. This is because Salvo, Nico and Lainy burst through the entrance.

"We're here!" yelled Nico. "And Lainy has your wedding dress!"

Everyone stopped moving. Salvo made his way through the packed bodies to the counter. He said a few words to the sergeant. They seemed to know each other. The cop smiled, laughed and waved his hand in the air.

I was absolutely baffled.

Salvo turned back to me. "Sergeant Doherty here says you can use the interview room to change, Gina. I'll stay here and complete the paperwork."

"I can go?" I said hopefully.

Bill grunted. He let go of his end of the bra. "Seems you have some big-shot relations in town who will vouch for you. They say it's all a mistake."

"It is," I said, nodding my head. "A case of mistaken identity." In fact, it was identity theft. But I didn't want to waste any more time explaining. I had a wedding to get to!

"There should be just enough time to make it to the chapel," said Nico, practically bouncing up and down. "Go, go, go!" He pointed to the little room.

Lainy rushed into the room first. I dashed to the doorway, then turned back. I looked over at topless Shirley and waved. She winked back.

The room had a few chairs, a steel desk and no window. I dropped my purse and cell phone down on the desk and undressed in record time. As I wiggled into the flowing gown, my cell phone binged again.

I pointed to it. "Hand that to me," I said to Lainy. "It's important."

The email was from Frank Portobello himself. It put a big fat smile on my face. "I think my little problem has just been solved," I said.

"Tell me," said Lainy.

"Stoner found the person who has been impersonating me," I said.

"What? How?" she asked.

"He hacked into Sugar Daddy dot com. Then he isolated the ip address of the computer used to create my fake account. Tracked it down to a street address right here in Vegas."

I slipped the cell phone into my purse and turned around to be zipped up.

"Wow! That's terrific. Is he going to tell the police here?" Lainy finished zipping.

"Oh, I don't think that will be necessary. That email was from Frank. He said he would take care of it. In fact, I think it's being handled at this very moment."

I didn't know exactly *how* he would handle it. One thing I've learned in this family is you don't need to know everything.

"That makes sense," said Lainy. "Frank believes in keeping family problems in the family. There's something of the Wild West about him."

I would remember to thank him later. At least the nightmare of identity theft would be over for me. Not only that, but this con artist wouldn't be hurting any other innocent people in the near future. That made me feel good.

Nico would be glad to hear all this. I'd tell him as soon as we were out of here. Pete—well, Pete didn't have to know everything, at least not now. Why spoil a perfectly good honeymoon?

I turned around. Lainy smiled her approval. "You look sensational."

"So do you," I said. Her country-and-western bridesmaid dress gleamed with rhinestones. Lainy was doing me proud.

"Ready to rumble? The clock is a-ticking."

"Let's go!" I said.

I held up the skirt of my gown and left the interview room. Nico gave a loud wolf whistle. The front room exploded in clapping.

My new friend whooped. I was relieved to see she was back in bra and T-shirt.

"Bye, Shirley! Thank you!" I said.

"You're welcome, honey! Gawd, you look like a million bucks."

I blew her a kiss from the door.

FOURTEEN

We made it to the outdoor chapel. Pete was waiting just inside the entrance, wearing a black tux and a big grin. "Just in time, gorgeous. And you really are gorgeous." His eyes roved over me.

"Sorry I'm late. I got detained." Probably I should leave it at that. He didn't need to know the why and where of it. "Don't tell me you were worried."

He drew me into a hug. "Babe, I will always worry about you. Comes with the territory."

I smothered a giggle on his shoulder. He didn't know the half of it.

We were married under an arbor of pink climbing roses and tacky Christmas lights. Lainy stood at my left. Nico was to Pete's right. The preacher was not an Elvis look-alike. In fact, she looked a lot like a smiling version of Aunt Miriam. This made me stand up straighter.

I forced myself to act serious and say the right words. Pete did the same. Apparently, we passed the test and were pronounced husband and wife. We passed the kissing part too.

"Golly shucks, Gina, you're married!" said Lainy. Nico whooped.

I could hardly believe it.

Pete gazed down at me with that look that makes me melt. "Hello, Mrs. Malone."

I grinned. "Hey! I can change my name now! Glory be!" Maybe all this identity theft would be behind me now.

Pete guided me away from the arbor. Then he reached down and wrapped his big arms around me.

"Aw," said Lainy. "You guys are so cute."

"Gina, I hate to break this up," said Nico, looking down at his cell phone. "But we should get back to the Necropolis now."

"Why?" I said. "What's the hurry?"

"Em…" Nico looked away from me and over to Pete. "It was sort of a last-minute plan, but Pete said it would be okay. Frank wanted to do something for you on your wedding day. So Salvo reserved a small dining room off the main one in the Necropolis. I said we'd be there by five o'clock. Don't want to keep the chef waiting."

"Well, that's a nice surprise," I said, happily clutching Pete's arm. "Will Frank be there?" I couldn't quite call him Dad yet.

Nico hesitated. "He might put in an appearance."

We made our way out of the chapel garden. Lighted angels in a riot of color lined the little laneway that led to the street.

"I call that dang decent of him," said Lainy. "Sugar, you gotta admit he's treating you well. Now that he knows about you."

I remembered the Elvis painting and smiled. Just how much would be in that Swiss bank account? And should I tell Pete about it? Maybe not. At least, not until after I talked to Frank. There was too much I didn't know. Not to mention, the less Pete knew about family business, the happier he would be.

Nico's cell phone rang. "Yes, yes," he said. "Okay." He clicked off and looked over at me.

"Frank wants us to take a detour. There's someone he wants you to meet."

I shot a glance to Pete.

"So we take a detour," said Pete. "If you think I'm letting you out of my sight..." He reached around my shoulders with one big arm and gave me a side hug.

Nico hailed a cab, and the four of us piled in.

We whizzed through the streets of downtown Vegas. At a stoplight, we turned right into a bedroom community that looked as if it had been around since Elvis was in school.

The cab pulled up in front of a small, shabby bungalow. A black SUV was parked in the driveway. One of Frank's henchmen—Ricky, I think—stood on the dilapidated front porch. He walked up to our cab as we came to a halt. I rolled down a window.

"Just Gina and Nico," he said. "The rest of you stay here."

I could feel Pete tense beside me. "It's okay," I said. "He's my father, remember? He won't let anything happen to me."

"Don't be long," Pete grumbled.

I scrambled out as well as I could in the designer wedding dress.

"Ick, gravel. Pick up the hem, Gina," said Nico. I did just that, pulling the skirt up to my knees. We scurried along after Ricky. Up the concrete steps, through the front door and then immediately down a narrow flight of stairs to the basement.

It took a few seconds for my eyes to adjust to the gloom. Frank was standing next to a steel computer desk. He grinned at me and gestured with his hand. "Meet your impostor," he said.

A high-school-age girl sat at the desk. Her eyes went wide when she saw me. "You're Gina? The real Gina?" Her young face blazed with delight. "You're so pretty." She said it breathlessly. Almost with a little hero worship in her voice, if I wasn't mistaken. Like she knew about my history. I glared at Frank.

"Thought you'd want to see for yourself," Frank said. "Your impostor is a sixteen-year-old girl working out of a basement." He sounded amused.

"Totally awesome," said Nico, clapping his hands together. "A mini Mini Mags. Gina, she's following in your footsteps."

I gulped. I didn't want to be that sort of role model. "What's your name, honey?" I said.

"Honey," she said. She even giggled. "On account of my hair color."

Holy cannoli. I'd been scammed by Nancy Drew's twisted sister.

"She wanted to meet you. On account of you were the brains who sussed her out," said Frank.

"*Sixteen?*" I shook my head. "So young." What a talent. That kid had some career ahead of her.

"Yeah. I thought the same. Shame to let a clever kid like that go to jail," he said. "So I made a deal. She's coming to work for us."

Nico rolled his eyes. "You made her an offer she couldn't refuse."

"Yeah. To the mutual benefit of all."

There was only one thing to do. I invited Honey to join us for the wedding dinner back at the hotel. She could travel with Frank. They liked that idea a lot. In retrospect, I didn't know if this was a good thing or a bad thing, but I couldn't stop to think about it. I had something more important to worry about.

What the heck was I going to tell Pete, who was waiting not so patiently in the car?

★ ★ ★

I left the explaining to Nico. He managed to tell a sanitized version that left out the televised news story and our trip to the police station. When Nico got to the Ernie and Jerry part, Pete even laughed out loud. That was a good sign. Of course, actually getting married might have had something to do with Pete's good mood. It certainly was responsible for mine.

It was a relief to know the nightmare would soon be over. There remained one potential problem. This deal Frank had worked with Honey was under the radar. The police would still be looking for the other Gina Gallo. Would I be stopped at the airport when I tried to board the plane to Canada?

That got me thinking about Mario, the doofus cousin who had gotten me into this mess. My hands automatically curled into fists.

★ ★ ★

Ten minutes later we were back in the lobby of the Necropolis. Nico led the way to the restaurant, past the zombies and morticians. The place was crowded, but no one seemed to be paying attention to me. I was old news, thank goodness. Of course, Lainy was with us, and she drew every eye. Even zombies seemed to part for her.

Nico led us into the Crematorium Grill. Never would I get used to that name. He paused in front of a closed door immediately to the right of the entrance, then backed away a bit.

"You two go first," he said to me.

Pete grabbed the gargoyle handle and swung the door open. I took one step into the dining room and stopped dead. Pete made a weird sound beside me.

The room was not empty. In fact, it was overflowing with bodies. Live ones.

"Surprise!" yelled Nico behind me.

There were Rita and Salvo. Uncle Vince and Sammy. Aunt Pinky, Aunt Griz and—gulp—Aunt Miriam. Vera, Vito and the gang from the Holy Cannoli Retirement Villa. Cousin Luca was pouring champagne for cousin Del. The entire Hammer family was there, and a few more besides. All wearing fancy duds and grinning. All talking at once. One voice rose above the crowd.

"Yay! Gina got married, and he isn't a putz," yelled Mad Magda.

The room erupted into cheers and claps. Nico's new girlfriend, Danny, ran forward to be with him. My cousin Tiff smothered me with a great big hug. The other aunts crowded in behind.

Pete did that donkey-snort thing again.

"Just wanted you to know," said Tiff, leaning in to speak quietly, "our in-house forger is creating a new passport for you under a different name. It will be delivered to this hotel by Express Post. Nico arranged it all this afternoon. You won't have any trouble getting back through customs."

"Oh, my god! That's wonderful. This whole party is wonderful!" I said with a grin.

"Isn't it?" said Nico, linking arms with Danny. "Lainy and I planned it as soon as I found out where you were going. Uncle Vince chartered a plane. Everyone is here except your mother and Phil, who got caught in that ice storm. But they'll be here by midnight."

"Everyone?" I said to Nico. "Even Mario?"

"Hi, Gina!" I saw Mario waving madly from the back of the room.

"Uh-oh," said Nico. "Pete, you might want to—"

"Mario, I'm going to kill you!" I yelled. I was going to kill him, all right. I was going to clobber him and bury him right here in the Necropolis. Then I was going to dance on his grave.

I kicked off my high heels, ready to launch at him. Pete clamped both hands down on my shoulders.

"Hey, babe. Not until after the reception."

"I'll reception you into the next century!" I yelled after Mario.

But he was already gone.

ACKNOWLEDGMENTS

This is Gina Gallo's sixth adventure, and I'm extremely grateful to the people who have provided encouragement and support for the series. Front of the pack are the deadly dames: Cathy Astolfo, Janet Bolin, Alison Bruce, Nancy O'Neill and Joan O'Callaghan, who serve as my beta readers. You rock!

I couldn't write comedy without the people who value it. Cheryl Freedman, Don Graves and Jeannette Harrison are always there to cheer me on. Thank you, dear friends.

I've been so lucky to have Ruth Linka and her team at Orca Book Publishers produce these books. They take my manuscript and make it better, every single time. Warm thanks to you all.

Billed as the "Queen of Comedy" by the *Toronto Sun* and called "the Canadian literary heir to Donald Westlake" by *Ellery Queen Magazine*, MELODIE CAMPBELL achieved a personal best when *Library Digest* compared her to Janet Evanovich. Melodie got her start writing stand-up and has since been a banker, marketing director, college instructor, comedy writer and possibly the worst runway model ever. Winner of ten awards, Melodie has been both a finalist for and a winner of the Derringer and Arthur Ellis awards for crime writing. She has over two hundred publications, including a hundred comedy credits, forty short stories and seven novels. Her work has appeared in *Alfred Hitchcock Mystery Magazine*, *Star Magazine*, *Flash Fiction Magazine*, *Canadian Living*, the *Toronto Star*, the *Globe and Mail* and many more. Melodie lives in Oakville, Ontario. For more information, visit melodiecampbell.com.